The ^very Fairy Princess
TAKES THE STAGE

by Julie Andrews & Emma Walton Hamilton

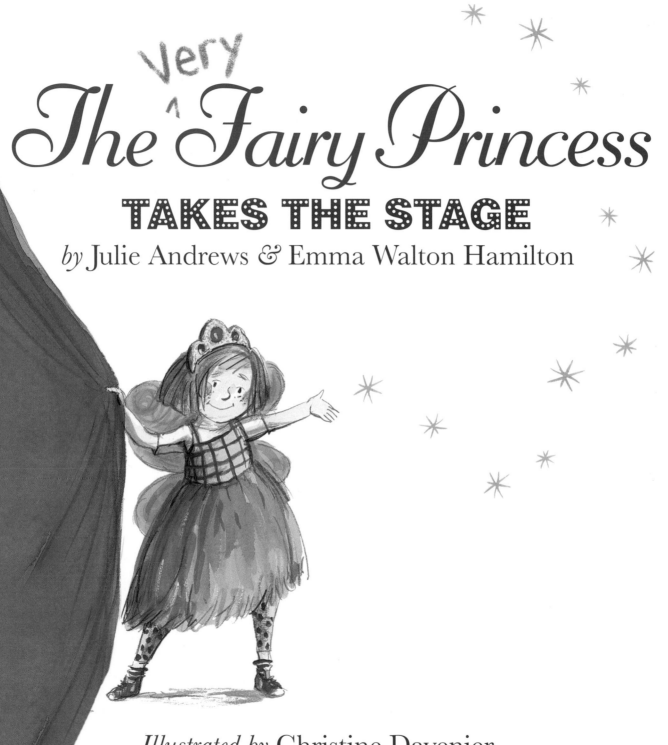

Illustrated by Christine Davenier

Little, Brown and Company

New York   Boston

Also, I do EVERYTHING that fairy princesses do.
I wear twirly dresses (with wings and a crown, of course), help
friends in need, and solve problems whenever and wherever I can.

Hi! I'm Geraldine.

I'm a fairy princess.

I know that I'm a fairy princess

because I FEEL it inside —

a sparkly feeling of just KNOWING in my heart.

But I REALLY let my sparkle out when I sing and dance!
(Fairy princesses have a LOT of flair.)

GUESS WHAT!

Madame Danielle, my ballet teacher, has made up a NEW show
for our spring performance! It's called *The Crystal Princess.*
I am PERFECT for the starring role because I already have the
costume AND the accessories!

And since I really AM a fairy princess, I'll be a natural.
(Fairy princesses are very practical.)

Unfortunately, Madame Danielle has a different idea.

She wants me to play the Court Jester because I am so *ebullient*.

I think that's a kind of soup, but she says it means "enthusiastic."

So I guess that's okay.

Tiffany gets to be the Crystal Princess.

She's a good dancer, and really pretty, but she doesn't have a CLUE how to be a princess. I give her some of my best tips, but she isn't very interested, and Madame Danielle reminds me there is room for only ONE ballet mistress in the company.

(Fairy princesses can sometimes be perfectionists!)

Mrs. Yamamoto brings in our costumes for a fitting.
Tiffany's dress is PERFECT...all shimmery and sparkly,
and it twirls around her when she spins. It has a matching crystal
tiara that twinkles in the light. Everyone makes a BIG fuss.

MY costume is a HUGE disappointment.

It's red and yellow (NOT my favorite colors, which are pink and purple).

It's VERY short.

It has a silly hat and pointy shoes with bells on them.

Worst of all, it makes me look like a BOY!

Mom says I'll look adorable anyway.
Dad says I'll always be HIS little princess, and my
brother, Stewart, says at least the tights will cover my
scabby knees. This doesn't make me feel any better.

A jester is sort of like a clown.

I have to hold a stick with a funny face on it,

so I pretend it's my fairy wand.

I also decide to wear my crown UNDER the silly hat.

(Fairy princesses never go ANYWHERE without a crown!)

On the night of the show, everyone is excited.
ESPECIALLY Tiffany.
I'm having a hard time finding my sparkle.

In the first dance,
I trip over my pointy shoes.

I throw in a few extra jetés to cover up, but
the bells on my silly hat are SO annoying!

Then I step on Tiffany's toe.
I do my best to keep smiling.
(A fairy princess has to keep her chin up, no matter WHAT!)

In the carnival scene — which is my BIG solo —
I drop my stick. When I bend to pick it up,
my crown slips out from under my hat!

I pirouette offstage, waving my arms
and pretending it's all part of the show.
But now I feel less sparkly than EVER.

At last, we get to the wedding scene, which is the "grand finale."
Tiffany walks down the aisle — step-together, step-together —
just like a perfect princess.
She looks GORGEOUS in her shimmery dress.
The music swells.

Ramone — who plays the prince — is waiting for her.

He lifts up her veil…and Tiffany's shining crystal tiara topples right off her head.

It clatters onto the stage. Then Ramone turns around and accidentally steps on it with a CRUNCH!

Everyone gasps.

Madame Danielle, who is playing the minister, is horrified.

Then she looks right at ME.

I put both hands on my head.

(Even a fairy princess finds it hard
to give up her most precious possession!)

But Tiffany looks SO sad. . . .
And a Crystal Princess REALLY needs to sparkle.
I know what I have to do.
(Fairy princesses are very intuitive.)

My crown fits Tiffany perfectly.
And the funny thing is, when I see her sparkling,
MY sparkle comes RUSHING back!

The wedding scene is a BIG hit.
The audience claps like crazy.
I can see Mom, Dad, and Stewart cheering.
I even spot my teacher, Miss Pym, in the audience!

During the curtain calls, Tiffany and I hold hands.
(Fairy princesses LOVE making new friends!)

When we take the company photograph,
Madame Danielle puts me in the very front.
Afterward, she gives me the jester's hat and
stick as souvenirs.
Tiffany gives me my crown back.
It feels EXTRA sparkly!

On the way home, Stewart tells me I was really cool in the show.

Mom keeps hugging me and stroking my hair.
Dad says, "I KNEW our very fairy princess would come through!"

I am so tired I can hardly keep my eyes open.
Daddy carries me to bed, and Mommy kisses me good night.

Just as I'm about to fall asleep,

I see my jester's hat on the bedpost.

One of the bells is sparkling in the moonlight.

Suddenly it doesn't seem like such a silly hat after all.

(Even a fairy princess is allowed to change her mind!)

For every fairy princess at heart.
—J.A. & E.W.H.

Pour Julie Andrews que j'admire et que j'aime depuis toujours et qui a
su apporter à ses personnages l'intelligence, l'espièglerie, la drôlerie et
le charme dont j'essaie de m'inspirer aujourd'hui pour donner vie
à notre merveilleuse petite Gerry!
—C.D.